TiBBLE AND GRANDPA

To Robert – I couldn't have written this
book without you or your compassionate
way of playing 'Top Threes'. .

W.M.

For Sudha.

D.E.

OXFORD
UNIVERSITY PRESS

Great Clarendon Street, Oxford OX2 6DP

Oxford is a registered trade mark of
Oxford University Press in the UK and in certain other countries

Text copyright © Wendy Meddour 2019
Illustrations copyright © Daniel Egnéus 2019

The moral rights of the author and illustrator have been asserted
Database right Oxford University Press (maker)

First published 2019

Data available
ISBN: 978-0-19-277195-7

1 3 5 7 9 10 8 6 4 2

Printed in China

Supported using public funding by

ARTS COUNCIL
ENGLAND

ARTS COUNCIL
ENGLAND

TIBBLE AND GRANDPA

WENDY MEDDOUR

DANIEL EGNÉUS

OXFORD
UNIVERSITY PRESS

Tibble was talking . . .

But Grandpa was
gardening.
Again.

Tibble went to
find Mum.

'Why's Grandpa
always
gardening?'
he asked.

'Just give him
time,' said Mum.

So Tibble gave Grandpa six-and-a-half minutes.

'Grandpa. Will you come and play trains with me, please?'

But Grandpa didn't hear.

'Grandpa's ears aren't working,' said Tibble.

Mum sighed. 'Ask him if he'd like a sandwich?'

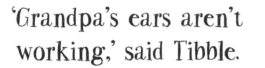

'GRANDPA, WOULD YOU
LIKE A SANDWICH?'
yelled Tibble.

Grandpa
made a little
grunty noise.

So Tibble tried again.

'Grandpa, what are your top three sandwiches?'

Grandpa said nothing.

'Mine are chocolate spread, raspberry jam, and butter with grated cheese,' said Tibble.

Grandpa looked at
Tibble and sighed.

'Salmon paste,' he said.

Tibble grinned.
'What about second
and third place?'

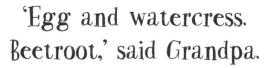

'Egg and watercress.
Beetroot,' said Grandpa.

Tibble ran off to make
Grandpa's Top Threes.

Tibble and Grandpa ate their
Top Threes by the pond.

'Grandpa, what are your Top
Three Jellyfish?' asked Tibble.

'Mine are moon jellyfish,
the upside down jellyfish,
and the one that looks like a
lion's mane,' said Tibble.

Grandpa licked the
beetroot off his fingers.

'Box jellyfish.
Compass jellyfish.
Portuguese man-of-war,'
he said.

After lunch, Grandpa watched as Tibble drew his
Top Three Jellyfish at the kitchen table.

Then, Grandpa joined in and played with Tibble's Top Three Trains.

'Thank you for not gardening,' said Tibble.

Grandpa ruffled Tibble's hair.

The next morning, Grandpa popped
his head round Tibble's door.

'Top Three Days Out?'
he asked.

Tibble jumped out of bed. 'The zoo.
The swimming pool. The park.'

Grandpa winked.

'Better get dressed then, lad.'

Tibble and Grandpa
went to the zoo.

They went swimming.

And they played
on the swings.

'My Top Three Animals
were gorillas, hippos,
and elephants,'
Tibble beamed.

'Penguins. Lions.
Giraffes,' said
Grandpa.

Grandpa and
Tibble smiled.

That night, they got out Tibble's telescope.
It had been a present from Granny.

'Who are your Top Three Grannies?'
asked Tibble.

Grandpa didn't answer.

'Mine are Granny who is dead.
Granny Agnes who lives on top of the shoe shop.
And the Granny in Little Red Riding Hood.'

Grandpa took a deep breath.

'Mine are Granny
when she danced
in the moonlight.

Granny when she
watered the roses . . .

. . . and Granny when
she first held you.'

'I miss Granny,' said Tibble.

'So do I, lad,' sighed Grandpa.

Then, Grandpa tucked Tibble up in bed.

'What were Granny's
Top Three Stars?' asked Tibble.

Grandpa smiled and kissed Tibble's head.

'That's easy, lad. Granny's Top Three Stars
were the Sun, the North Star, and . . .

'YOU.'